BLACK

KNIGHT

OF

BERKELEY

Nathaniel Robert Winters

BUFFALO PRINTING COMPANY
Napa Valley California

Copyright 2015 Nathaniel R. Winters

This work of fiction was inspired by
three other works of fiction, Camelot,
Ivanhoe and The Shadow radio
shows.

Those heroes and villains of earlier
generations come alive again in this
novel. I am thankful for the ideals of
chivalry. It gives us some principles
to strive for, especially in the barbaric
times in which we live.

Nathaniel Robert Winters 2015

Chapter 1   Man in Shadows

He was invisible, just another shadow in the darkness, dressed head-to-toe in black, hiding, waiting for the dream to reappear. He'd seen it, all too clearly, in his dream.

Were they dreams or nightmares?

He knew this was the place it would happen.

One hour from midnight he'd seen her emerge from the BART station. She walked quickly, heels clicking on the sidewalk. Her assailant was now behind her, just feet away, the dark skin of both almost invisible in the blackness of night.

In another moment the knife would be at her throat.

The movement was quick, never leaving the shadows. His cane came down on the back of the assailant's neck. The man fell, knife clanging bell-like on the sidewalk. She saw his shadow moving quickly away, and knew he had saved her.

"Who are you?"

She heard his doppler voice. "I am the black of night."

Kathy Linden didn't stop running until she was safe in her apartment. Then she called 911. Berkeley Police found an unconscious man and his knife on the Shattuck Street sidewalk.

The assault was recorded on the back pages of the **Chronicle** and the end of the local newscasts.

She called him *The Black Knight*. In his dream, her death and her blood spilled across the front pages of the newspaper and the beginning of the local newscasts.

Chapter 2   Swinging the Night Away

One year earlier, Ivan Duncan, Gulf War veteran, taught history and coached basketball at Berkeley High. The Cal graduate was bright and popular with students and faculty. Students waited in line to get into his tough Western Civilization classes.

His basketball teams were constant winners and playoff contenders.

Still single at 36, friends were always trying to fix him up with just the right girl. He laughed at their suggestions and said he was married to his job. Yet he was often seen about town with a variety of pretty women.

On the evening that would change his life, Ivan's date was a raven-haired beauty named Gwen Fisher. Ivan was actually enamored with the girl. Her Eurasian look reminded him of his mother. Gwen also had a casual sophistication that had stolen his attention. That night, she wore a simple pink T-shirt, comfortable tennis shoes with pink socks that matched the shirt. Jeans hugged her derrière. A gold chain shimmered on her neck.

They were talking about the Middle East. Ivan said, "There will never be peace there. Seems somebody's always fighting someone else."

Gwen bit her lip, an unconscious habit while in serious conversation.

He thought it was cute. "It was hard for you over there, wasn't it?" she said.

Ivan looked away, not holding her gaze. "Hard and frustrating. What good did it do?"

"You were there before…"

"Yes, before."

What was left unsaid was the attack on the Trade Towers. She knew he had lost both his parents on that day, causing darkness in his usual sunshiny personality.

"I was a student at Cal then, watched it all unfold on TV," he said.

She reached out for his hand and pulled him back from his daydream and into the room.

Come on," he said, "let's get out of here. How about dancing? I want to dance."

"Yeah, sounds good, let's dance. I heard the club down the street is having a throwback Forties' style big band."

"Yeah," he said. "The Forties, when we knew what we were fighting for. Do you know how to jitterbug?"

"Don't they make Raid to kill those jitterbugs?" She laughed.

"Don't say anything. I know it's a dance."

***

They took a break after a couple of Rum and Cokes, cha cha's and mambo's. The band broke into, *It Don't Mean A Thing if It Ain't Got That Swing*, " dowop dowop…" The horns blared.

She grabbed his hand and said "Come on, we gotta dance to this!"

They were swingin' and sweatin' when it hit him.

He fell to the floor like he'd been shot and lay there shaking, his face covered with a thin film of cold sweat.

Gwen screamed out "Help! Somebody call 911! Please!"

She could hear the siren screaming, screaming out a warning. She's thinking, why is it taking so long?

An instant later, the ambulance arrived. EMT's were all over him, a respirator surrounding his face. Then he was on a gurney and gone.

A shadow seemed to have darkened her world. Gwen shivered like a cold hand was gripping her. She even forgot to ask where they were taking him. She sat at the table, too shocked to move.

Ivan had told her he had no living relatives in California. The band restarted and played on, as tears rolled down her face.

Even though Gwen and Ivan did not have a serious relationship, she felt somewhat responsible for him, believing their dancing had somehow caused his body to malfunction.

She called the local hospitals until she found out that he was lying in a coma at Highland Hospital in Oakland.

Chapter 3   Lion Hearted

Rich De Leone was a big man. Six foot six inches of mostly muscle. His father had played football for the New York Jets. Rich had played power forward on the Cal basketball team with Ivan Duncan. Since then they had been best friends. On the court and off, they fit like coffee and cream.

After graduating with a degree in engineering, Rich went to work for Apple computers, developing hardware to improve computer memory chips. Jumping on the Silicon Valley bandwagon, he started his own company, making and supplying top-of-the-line memory chips and computer-brain interface hardware.

Rich's company, SmartWare, was developing an experimental computer chip that could be implanted into the brain of a patient developing Alzheimer's disease.

With world-class UCSF brain surgeon Merle "The Wizard" Doggs, Rich felt like he was close to making a breakthrough with his most recent iteration. Dr. Doggs had gained vast experience doing the latest type of Deep Brain Stimulation (DBS) surgery on Parkinson's patients.

Despite intense computer testing of their brain chip, a major problem for Rich and Dr. Doggs was the refusal of the FDA to allow testing on a real living human brain.

Rich heard about Ivan's massive aneurism from Gwen, who

had been calling Ivan's friends, using his cell phone's call list. Strangely, Rich's sadness was mixed with hopeful goosebumps. He felt like fate was knocking on his door.

Immediately, he called Dr. Merle Doggs and explained Ivan's critical condition.

"I want to get a first-hand look at him here at UCSF," said Merle. "Who do we see to get him transferred?"

"Ivan has no living relatives or family in California. The woman who called me was just his date for the night. I'm actually his best friend and closest confidante," said Rich.

Merle told Rich it would be hard to get medical approval to move Ivan and asked if his SmartWare brain chip project was ready for human testing.

"Ready and waiting," said Rich. "Don't you see this was meant to be?"

"I'm not sure about that fate thing, but it seems like an opportunity. Let's get him transferred first," said Merle.

"Remember, you're the expert here. Nobody's going to question you," said Rich.

"What are you implying?" Merle said.

"We can implant the chip and keep it between us, a secret."

"You want to put my medical license on the line?" said Merle.

"No FDA, no feds, and no bureaucrats – the more we keep them out of this, the faster we can work to save Ivan. It would take the FDA five years to approve this. Merle, I'm fighting to save the life of my best friend."

Merle was tempted, his resistance dissolving, breaking down. "You're right . . . your friend Ivan would be long dead before they'd approve it."

***

Dr. Doggs met the patient coming in on an ambulance transfer from Highland Hospital. Doggs danced Ivan's gurney past intake, commanding nurses and orderlies like a general. Ivan was swept into a private room with one of Dr. Doggs' team nurses. "I want an MRI, blood work, EKG, stat. I'm expecting a FedEx medical delivery from SmartWare tomorrow. Send it directly to my lab. Schedule my surgical team for this patient, Wednesday at 6 AM."

Rich De Leone blew in right behind the patient and went directly up to the sleek, well-equipped lab of his cohort Dr. Merle Doggs, a lab which he knew quite well.

"I scheduled the surgery for 6 AM Wednesday," said Merle.

"Here's a sample of the chip," said Rich, slipping a tiny glassine envelope from his vest pocket. "I've got it down to the size of a fingernail. When a new battery is needed, a subdural wire has leads, behind the ear lobe. You know that huge controller that goes under the skin for DBS? In this version, it is now integrated into the chip itself. We program it wirelessly – like DBS – with a little gadget like a TV remote," said Rich.

"Your technology has come a long way, Rich -- fast. I can tell any

curious medical personnel on my
operating team that I'm putting in an
experimental stent – anyway, that's
what it will look like on an MRI,"
said Merle.

Chapter 4   Strange Dreams

Ivan dreams, not like a fuzzy black of night dream, but a terrifyingly bright Technicolor dream.

The towers, the two World Trade Center towers, standing there, upright twins. Then the plane hits Tower One piercing its hard outer shell.

His parents were having breakfast at Windows on the World.

Ivan's father, Winston, was an English Literature professor at Columbia.

He'd worked his way out of the Bronx projects by winning a scholarship to Yale.

His mother, a Siberian émigré, was one of Calvin Klein's top runway models, then a **Sports Illustrated** swimsuit cover girl. After working her way through NYU, she'd created a spot for herself as a Wall Street investment analyst.

Fifteen minutes later, the second plane hits Tower Two. The

towers fall to the ground like cracked eggs. Yolk and egg whites spilling like blood, those fragile broken eggs.

All of America's advanced technology couldn't put them back together again.

He wakes, the world coming back to him groggily. Out of the depths of the dream, he sees his buddy Rich De Leone. He hears, vaguely, "Ivan." He tried to answer but his mouth was full of marbles and dry, dry. No saliva. Tried to say "Rich" again. This time a squeak came out. Finally, he heard a shaky baritone come out of his mouth, saying "jjjjjjjjjjjoooooooccee."

Rich said "Ivan, I'm here for you buddy. Are you all right?"

Ivan whispered, "wwwaaaaaaater, wwwaaaaater, so dry, thirrrsty."

"I can give you ice," said Rich. "Suck it slowly."

Ivan's mouth came alive like the desert sand under a spring rain.

"Wwwwwaaaat, wwwwaat hhhapppennnned?"

"You've been through quite a trauma, buddy," said Rich. "But we've assembled quite a surgical team for you here. We think you're going to be OK."

Ivan laid there thinking... before that nightmare of a dream, I was dancing with Gwen, was it in Berkeley? How did I get in this hospital room? He knew the questions would be answered later. It was nice to see Rich at his side. It gave him confidence. If there was one man you wanted to be in a foxhole with, it was Rich De Leone.

He took inventory. There were tubes coming out of both arms, IV bags hanging on both sides of the bed. His head felt strange but the pain was negligible. Rich held a cup of ice chips to Ivan's mouth. He realized his hands were tied to gates on the sides of his bed. He felt like a dog wearing a cone hat to keep from scratching. Finally, he was able to ask the question.

"Rich. What happened?"

Rich gave it to him straight. "You had an aneurism, a clot in your brain. I have a lot to fill you in on, but that will have to wait until later. My friend, Dr. Merle Doggs, thinks you're out of the woods. You're going to be okay, buddy."

Ivan drifted back to sleep. Perchance to dream those awful dreams.

***

Fog filtered the San Francisco sun, shadowy light beams through the window of the ICU. Ivan's eyes slowly open. He'd had another awful dream but he can't quite bring out the memory.

A smiling nurse came bedside and said "How are *we* feeling today, Ivan?"

We, he thinks to himself, we? "I feel like I've been run over by an M1 tank tread." He smiles. "How are you feeling, bet no tanks ran over you last night."

The nurse laughs. "I guess I'm feeling a little better than you. How's your head?"

"Strangely, it feels pretty good. It's the rest of me that doesn't feel so great."

"That's good," said the nurse. "That's normal. Your body's going to have to work itself back to strength. Your brain's been through quite a trauma. Dr. Doggs will be making rounds shortly. He's going to explain what happened. Are you hungry?"

"I could eat," he said. "I'll have two cheeseburgers and a chocolate milk shake please. And make that to go."

"Seems like you've got your sense of humor," said the nurse. "How about some Jello and some Cream of Wheat for starters?"

"You're going to be no fun, are you," said Ivan.

"Yep, a regular Nurse Rachet. Excuse me while I change your catheter. I'll wash my hands before I bring you your gruel."

Dr. Doggs walks in, brighter than the foggy UCSF sunshine. "So how are we today," he asks.

Ivan thinks *we*, again with the we? What is this we stuff? "Did you have surgery on your head also?"

"Point taken," said Merle. "How are **you** feeling?"

"I've felt better."

"Care to be specific? I am your doctor. How's your head?"

"Head feels pretty good. It's the rest of me I'm not sure about. What the hell did you do to me?"

Merle said, "I'm waiting for your friend Rich. We have some things to tell you."

Rich whisked into the room. "Sorry I'm late, Ivan. I was in a meeting. But I'm here now and I have something very important and secret to tell you.

I want to give it to you straight. You deserve it."

"Uh, OK," said Ivan. "What's going on?"

Rich said "Dr. Doggs here saved your life. He's one of the best surgeons in the country. You had a major aneurism in your brain. Parts of your brain were destroyed."

"Really? My thinking isn't all that bad."

Rich said, "That's the secret part. I invented a new computer chip that can do a lot of the thinking for you. It won't change your personality. But it might make you smarter."

Ivan said "You know that's not possible. Seriously, Rich, is this for real?"

"You're the first person to get the chip," said Rich. "That's why it's a secret. If we'd let the bureaucrats get in the way, you'd be dead by now. So do not, this is very important, do not tell anybody."

Ivan said "I'm glad it was you, Rich. If it was anybody else, I'd be worried."

Dr. Doggs said "Ivan, you can call me Merle – we're going to be working closely together. The good

news is your body's in great shape.
You just have to recover from the
surgery. And we'll put you on a
physical therapy schedule. Any
questions?"

"One comes to me right away.
Does it affect my dreams?"

"Well, we'll see, won't we,"
said Rich. "We have a program
controller that can tone it down, if
need be."

"Does it affect the energy level
of my body?"

"It shouldn't," said Dr. Doggs.
"When you recover from the surgery

and get stronger from the physical therapy, you should be fine."

"Does anybody else know about this?" said Ivan.

"No," Merle answered, "Just the three of us. It's got to be our secret. The FDA knows we've been working on a chip for Alzheimer patients, but it's a long way from their approval. You don't have Alzheimer's, so you may be a better or a worse candidate. We don't know."

Ivan laughs. "Any super powers?"

"I'm afraid you're just going to have to go with the body you've got. But you played ball in college, right?"

"Yeah, I passed the ball a lot to this big lug next to you," said Ivan. "He never missed within ten feet."

"That's good. Sense of humor, and you're athletic. I think you'll need both."

Chapter 5   Uncle David

Ivan continued having strange dreams. It was almost like his life was replaying itself. In his next dream, he was five years old, back in his families' Greenwich Village townhouse. It was gently snowing outside, the fire was in the hearth and a tall Christmas tree stood in the living room. His mom and dad were so young.

Dad handed him a present to open. He tore through the wrapping and pulled his first basketball out of the box.

"Wow, just what I wanted. Oh man, can I play with it today?

"No son, your grandmother and Uncle Dave are coming over. It's snowing," said Mom. "Go upstairs. I laid out some clothes for you."

"Mom, not that wool sweater. You know wool scratches me and gives me the heebie-jeebies."

"It's Christmas. You can wear that nice sweater your grandmother

gave you for just this one day. And
you can change out of it as soon as
everybody leaves."

"Oh, okay."

His mother laughed. "Come on
now Ivan, it's Christmas, make your
mother happy."

"Yeah, but remember, I'm
taking that sweater off as soon as
everyone leaves."

Ivan's Uncle Dave arrived
from the Bronx with his mother,
Ivan's grandmother. David had never
moved out or moved up from the
projects and had a shady reputation.

Ivan's father begged Dave to please be on his best behavior for their mother for Christmas.

"Sure," Dave said brimming with sarcasm, "Anything for my big brother."

Even young Ivan smelled the booze on his uncle's breath and knew the peace wouldn't last very long. His father and his Uncle Dave were always arguing. Dave called his older brother a sellout.

Uncle Dave had started drinking early. Dave tossed Ivan a present. Ivan ripped open the paper and found a Barbie doll in stilettos and bikini. Everyone stared, silent, aghast.

"What's the mattah?" said Dave. "It looks just like the kid's mom before she got married."

Winston just shook his head. "Dave, you're drunk already. Why don't you just leave? I'll take mom home."

"Yeah, you fuckin' Oreo. You just think you're too good for me."

David slammed the door on his way out. An avalanche of snow slid down from the roof, burying him in cold wet fluff, chilling the heat under his collar.

"Mothahfukkah!" he yelled.

Chapter 6   Land's End

"You still dreaming in
technicolor?" Rich asked his friend.

"I dream about daytime stuff in
color and nights in both dayglow
color plus black and white. Why?"
said Ivan.

"I've been working on a
computer simulation to turn it down.

"No, don't.

I have an intuition that these dreams actually reset my memories, that they're important."

"Okay, but let me know if they get too intense."

That day Ivan was transferred to the VA hospital, ending his stay in the secret room at UCSF and facing people for the first time after brain aneurism surgery.

"How do you think he's doing?" Rich asked Doctor Merle.

"Great, considering he should be dead," said Merle.

The old San Francisco Veterans Administration hospital was located on an immensely valuable, special piece of ground. It sat high atop a hill at Land's End, where San Francisco Bay meets the ocean, west of the Golden Gate Bridge. Though the spot was always fogged in during summer, Ivan's November stay yielded spectacular views. Land's End was a great place to start walking and building back his muscle strength. The VA also offered a rehabilitation room fitted with weights and cardiovascular machines which he used often.

That day, he also had his first outside visitor. Gwen arrived. She was surprised and happy to see him up and out of bed. They went for a walk on a trail just below the hospital that led to the Cliff House Restaurant.

"You're looking quite well, I'm glad to see," she said.

"Yes, I've had the best of care. Good news, Dr. Doggs said I'm going to live," he said tongue in cheek. "You may get to dance with me yet.

Gwen, I'm very thankful for what you did," he continued. "If you hadn't called Rich, who's friends with Dr. Doggs, I wouldn't be alive today."

"Was my dancing so bad it caused your brain to explode?" she said with a smile.

"It appears that way," he said, smiling back. He kissed her on the cheek. "Gwen, I really like you a lot. But with my health so unsteady, I don't think it's time to start a relationship. Are you okay with that?"

"Sounds reasonable, but after your rehabilitation is over, you owe me a proper date."

"It's a deal," he said, and they shook hands. "Oh, what the hell." He kissed her. She kissed back, causing a zap in his brain electronics, at least that's what it felt like. "I hope that will hold you over until I'm out."

She giggled, "You just better get well soon. Okay?"

Gwen walked him back to his room. He was surprised at how much he missed her when she left.

Chapter 7   The Legend of Boarding School

Another night, another dream. This dream paraded through his preppy private high school. The dream was in technicolor again. He was one of the few black kids in his lily white Connecticut countryside boarding school. The racism he faced was subtle, with few of the students openly hostile to him. Many actually sought his friendship. The administration chose the only other black student as his roommate. He felt he belonged, like a palm tree in Brooklyn.

His parents were more concerned about his education then his comfort. They knew most city schools did not offer excellence. Ivan made the most of it, got outstanding grades, played point guard for the basketball team, and even learned how to fence like Zorro, something he would never learn in New York City schools.

To his total consternation, his Uncle David showed up at school the day after his 14th birthday in his pink Cadillac pimpmobile to take him for an after-school ride. Ivan found himself sitting next to a cute 16-year-old girl.

"I think it's time for you to become a man," said Uncle Dave. Then he dropped them off at the Garden Motel, Room 125. "I'll be back in two hours. Enjoy yourself."

"Listen, you don't have to do anything," Ivan assured the girl.

"Susan, my name is Susan. Don't feel guilty, it's not my first time. Dave pays me well, and it sure beats waiting tables in a grease pit, divey diner in the Bronx. Besides, you're kinda cute."

That was Ivan's introduction to sexual pleasure. When Uncle David dropped him off back at school he was already a legend. Six friends followed him back to his room, demanding every detail. He didn't tell much, just smiled a lot.

By the time he was a senior, every detail he'd never told was retold many different ways.

Ivan awoke from his dream, lustful, wishing almost desperately he was alone with Gwen.

Chapter 8   No Three Stooges

The three met almost every day. Merle checked Ivan's vital signs. Rich scanned and tested the chip. It was thumbs up all around.

"The only reason not to discharge you," said Merle, "is to keep an eye on how your brain and body react to that chip."

The aneurism surgery triumvirate were now tied together -- a special team. The three shared a secret of enormous importance with the potential of changing medical history.

The three of them went for their first walk together, on the cliffs below the VA. Could Rich, Merle and Ivan become future medical legends? Become another trio, like The Three Musketeers, the Marx Brothers, the magical Cub double-play combination of Tinker-to-Evers-to-Chance or the

Celtic's famed Larry Bird, Robert Parish, and Kevin McHale.

That glorious Sunday they were just three friends walking a spectacular trail. Directly ahead, the Golden Gate Bridge loomed large and the Pacific Ocean sparkled to their left. All of San Francisco lay to the right, its hills and cable cars reaching heavenward on that glorious sunshiny day.

Chapter 9   Harlem Shuffle

Rich and Merle went home, leaving Ivan to face the dreams of night, alone in his hospital room. That night's dream was an uncomfortable memory. Summer after his senior year, his Yale scholarship tucked firmly in his pocket, the boy was ready to follow in his father's footsteps, when fate, by the name of

Uncle David, stepped firmly in his way.

Uncle Dave invited him to lunch uptown on Harlem's 125th Street. They shared a big platter of soul food, piled high with barbecued ribs, fried chicken, beans and rice, each with their own fork.

Dave and Winston, Ivan's father, never got along but that didn't have to get in the way of uncle and nephew. They were having a good ol' time, Motown music pumping its beat from a colorful jukebox. Uncle Dave poured the boy a couple shots of whiskey and they went out back and smoked a fragrant joint. David offered to drive Ivan home.

"I don't think so," said Ivan.

"You've been drinking, and you know you and my dad don't get along. I'll just hop on the subway." They hugged and said goodbye.

Two cops were waiting at the underground entrance like they had been tipped off. "Hey kid, what's in your backpack?"

"Just some books."

The two officers went through his pack like drug sniffing dogs at an airport. A rival of Uncle Dave ratted his nephew out.

"What's this?" a cop asked, holding a half pound bag of marijuana above his head.

Ivan believed that Uncle David had given him a present for college, not knowing that one of his enemies had set the boy up. Ivan was eighteen, an adult in New York, and now facing a drug trafficking charge.

Ivan's father was forced to hire an expensive, top-flight attorney.

Considering Ivan's spotless record, the DA was willing to make a deal. Instead of five years in prison, Ivan could join the Army.

Gone was the scholarship to Yale. Hello Desert Storm.

Chapter 10   Endless War

Waking up in the VA hospital the next morning, Ivan felt sorry and sad. David had just been trying to do something nice, and an unknown rival had messed with him to get at David. Winston and Anastasia never talked to David again, blaming him for the destruction of Ivan's Yale education.

He hadn't seen his Uncle for a while and missed him. After making some calls, Ivan was floored to discover his uncle had been murdered just a month ago.

***

Veterans were all around him. The hospital felt more like a military than civilian institution.

The very next night he dreamed about the army. He was marching off to war in Desert Storm. As he marched, the uniforms changed to ancient Greeks marching in a phalanx, driving their long spears into the

Persians, pushing them back.
Suddenly he held a Roman short
sword, hacking an ancient Israelite.
Then, encased in full medieval armor
mounted on a great steed, he was a
Crusader charging a Muslim, in a line
of British Red Coats firing muskets at
Egyptians, then a Russian WW I
machine gunner blasting Turks, a
WW II Englishman, his rifle barking
at Rommel's Desert Rats, an Israeli
firing against Arabs, a Russian against
Afghanis, finally, Ivan back in his
own GI uniform, marching with his
American platoon in Desert Storm.

Gunshots rang out and the American platoon fell in a hail of lead. He was the last man standing.

Then he was back on his war horse, wrapped in black medieval armor, the black knight, lance and shield in hand.

He didn't wake immediately but stayed in that dreamlike-state between light and dark, a black knight? Where did that come from? What did it mean?

He didn't know, but felt that fate was trying to tell him something.

The next day, when he told Rich and Merle about his dream, they couldn't understand what the black knight meant either.

Rich reminded him, "I can turn your dreams down on your chip."

"No," Ivan said. "Something important is in these dreams. I know it."

Chapter 11   Butterfly Killer

Just about Thanksgiving, Ivan had his strangest dream yet. The dream started in the second grade. It was about a classmate.

Brian Boris Gilbert was raised by good, role model parents just a block from Ivan's home in Greenwich Village. Even as an eight-year-old, Ivan could tell something was wrong with this boy.

He cussed at the girls, even spit at them and laughed. He bullied the smaller boys. Ivan watched as Brian caught a butterfly and pulled its wings off, just to watch it die.

He started avoiding Brian, and noticed that the other kids also gave him a wide berth.

Brian was like a lemon you get at a Mercedes-Benz dealer. He looked good and dressed well, but nobody could ever fix him. As he got older he seemed to get even more evil. In sixth grade he bragged about killing old Blackie, his neighbor's cat. Ivan lost track of him when he went off to school in Connecticut.

In Ivan's dreams, he saw things he couldn't consciously know. The dreams started filling in the lost years. Brian had dropped out of school at 16 and started hanging around gangbangers.

Gilbert became proficient with a knife, first slitting a dog's throat, then cutting the throat of a rival gang member.

Then Ivan saw, it was Brian in Harlem, the day he lunched with his

Uncle Dave Duncan and then got busted for drugs at the subway.

Recognizing Brian from grade school in the Village, he wondered what his former classmate was doing so near Uncle David, a rival gang member.

Then, he saw in his dream, how Brian slipped the bag of pot into his school bag while he went to the restroom at lunch. Brian laughed out loud as he phoned the police and ratted out Ivan.

By the time of Ivan's brain surgery, Gilbert's murder count was

up to eight rivals and two prostitutes –
always with a knife and Ivan saw the
dying moment of each and every one
of them. This was a nightmare that
would stay with him.

But it was getting too hot for
Brian in New York.

He chose to make one last hit.
Gilbert snuck up behind David
Duncan just after dark with nobody
else around and stabbed him in the
back of the neck.

Ivan's uncle toppled, blood
oozing a day-glow red in his dream,

flowing, stream-like, down the dirty sidewalk.

Ivan's pounding heart jolted him awake. He was emotionally raw. How could he possibly dream things he knew nothing about? He somehow knew these things were real and had happened just like in his dream. What was he supposed to do with this revelation? Should he tell Rich and Merle about these surrealistic nightscapes? Ivan decided to hold off on divulging this dream to his two buddies.

Chapter 12   Rebecca

Before his release from the
hospital it was important that Merle
and Rich get a good baseline of Ivan's
mental capacity. During four hours of
grueling mind grinding testing, Ivan
met Rebecca Isaac, the psychologist.

The first thing he noticed about
Rebecca was her hair, deep brown,
flowing and curling to her waist. Her
face sported happy brown eyes and

when she smiled her glow somehow spread to others in the room. Her 35 years showed a light touch of crow's feet crinkling at her eyes. Even during the challenging tests, Ivan realized Rebecca had qualities he needed in a confidante.

As the test ended he asked, "Do you do private therapy?" She gave him her card and asked if he'd like to see her in a month or so.

"No," he said. "I need a good counselor, immediately."

"This baseline test will take a while to score, but if your need is immediate, I can spare you an hour this evening," said Rebecca.

Ivan laughed. "Doc, believe me, if we start, we're going to be more than an hour. And I think you're going to want to hear the full story. How about I order a pizza from Giovanni's down on Geary -- they make a good prosciutto and mushroom pizza. I'll buy, of course."

"Fine. Anything but anchovies."

Over pizza, Ivan asked, "Rebecca, do you believe in ESP

"My parents were hippyish, came to San Francisco from New York with flowers in their hair. I grew up in Marin, so of course I believe there are vibes out there we can't explain," Rebecca replied.

Ivan started telling her about his technicolor dreams.

Ivan told her about the microchip in his brain.

"You think I'm crazy?"

"Do you believe the part of that last dream, you couldn't possibly know?" said Rebecca.

He nodded. "It seems very real to me."

Rebecca took a deep breath. After a moment, she said, "I don't think you're crazy. But I do understand why you feel that you might need professional help. I'm also not sure the dreams can be taken verbatim -- they might symbolize something else. Either way, this is a lot for you to handle. How are you feeling?"

"A little better, after telling you, Rebecca. You are only the fourth person aware of my microchip and

my dreams. Please keep our
conversation confidential."

　　"Your secret is safe with me.
It's my professional duty," said
Rebecca. "See you next week?"

Chapter 13   Home

Ivan's release from the VA Hospital arrived one day before Thanksgiving.

Dr. Doggs signed off on his papers. The doctor gave him a clean bill of health. He told Ivan, "For a man who's had major brain surgery, you are in incredible physical shape."

"On the first MRI, dead sections were showing up because of

the massive cerebral event you experienced. The latest MRI shows no dead areas in the brain, meaning the chip is working perfectly with your cerebrum."

"Thank you," Ivan said.

Merle pointed to Rich. "Thank **that** guy. Without that chip, you'd be a goner."

Rich drove home to Los Gatos. Ivan planned to spend Thanksgiving with his buddy Rich and wife Rowena. They'd been married two years; no children yet. But, they claimed laughingly, it was not for lack of trying.

Ivan delighted in Rich's choice of a bride. Rowena was smart and pretty. He thought her British accent sounded dignified.

But being typically English, she was a terrible cook. Spice was a totally foreign concept; tastes better left to the French, or worse, the food of Asian Indians that had invaded London. Here in the South Bay there seemed an Indian restaurant on every corner. She got heartburn just driving down the street. So the boys volunteered to make the traditional American turkey dinner, with a big screen in the kitchen tuned in to football.

After the day's festivities, bellies full, Rich drove Ivan home to Berkeley.

Home! I'm actually home after all this time, he thought.

His modest two bedroom house in North Berkeley never looked so good. What should he do first?

"Gwen, call Gwen," he said out loud. My God what's that smell? His nose led him to the refrigerator and many months of spoiled food.

Gwen would have to wait.

Chapter 14   Brian Boris Gilbert

Saturday morning about 10 AM, the fateful knock sounded at the front door. Unannounced, Brian Gilbert arrived at his brother's apartment in Oakland where Tim lived inconspicuously with his girlfriend Tina.

Tim Gilbert lived in Oakland, California, a continent away from his malignant older brother.

It was now obvious he didn't go far enough away.

"Aren't you going to ask me in?"

It was more a command than a question.

"Sure, come in," said Tim.

Brian peered into the shabby studio apartment, then stepped across the threshold as if it were a pigsty. The gangster was dressed in a three-piece striped suit with shoes buffed to bright shine. He sneered at the bed on the floor and the secondhand furnishings. "You could have been livin' in New York, in style, with me." His face had the look of someone who had bitten into a sour pickle.

"Yeah, probably," said Tim. "But then I woulda' had to live near you."

"You need to show me respect, little brother."

"Why? Because you always beat the shit out of me when we were kids? I don't have to respect your sorry ass anymore. Get out of my house or I'll call the cops."

Knife found throat as the older brother's temper exploded. Blade moved so fast Tim never saw it coming. Death came almost as quickly.

"Dammit, I got blood on my new suit," said Brian.

He smiled cruelly at the shocked Tina. "Let's you and me have some fun."

Tina became like the butterfly whose wings he'd slowly pulled off as a six-year-old.

Brian paced himself, careful not to drink too much scotch out of his pocket flask. He wanted to stay sharp and focused on the job at hand, carving up his late brother's girlfriend. Brian the Blade tortured her for hours until the girl welcomed death.

Ivan saw it all in a nightmarish dreamland.

***

There is an old saying: Dead men tell no tales. But TV and newspaper reporters do and no tales were told. There was nothing in the papers, on TV, or on the radio news. Not even a whisper on an internet blog. Yet Ivan believed the dream. Why was there nothing - nothing about a crime involving a double murder? He didn't understand.

Chapter 15   Premonition

Rebecca studied Ivan as he told her his latest dream about Brian the Blade.

She saw a very attractive man in his late 30's, skin the color of coffee latte. She wondered, does the term African-American apply when one's mother is white?

It did for President Obama. She never liked African-American as a racial term. What if the person moved here from France?

Anyway, he sure is cute, she thought, with a rich chocolate tint to the curly hair now growing over the incision. One could not even tell he'd had brain surgery.

Knock it off Rebecca, she thought to herself, he is a client. Her concentration returned firmly to his nightmare. "Maybe this is a foreshadowing of something that hasn't happened yet."

He turned that over in his mind. It made perfect sense to him. "Maybe it's a premonition that I can do something about."

"Wait a darn minute," said Rebecca. "I wasn't suggesting you go off like Batman and take on a madman."

"Why else would I have the dream," he asked not only Rebecca, but himself.

Rebecca asked, "Do you trust Merle and Rich?"

"Absolutely, with my life."

"Maybe it's time to share this with them. They could help."

"I don't want them in danger."

"Are you the only one who chooses to face fate with free will?"

"You know just how to get to me, don't you?" he said, smirk of a smile on his face.

"That's why you pay me the big bucks, isn't it."

Before he left, he called his friends. Rebecca agreed to meet with them. He now had a team of four.

Chapter 16   Gunivere "Gwen" Fisher

Gwen Fisher worked for Channel 8 News, an independent Bay Area TV station. With a degree in journalism from UCLA she had hoped to get on a big city newspaper staff. Most papers were fighting a losing battle with the internet and were not hiring. But she had a face born to be on TV. She started on frill assignments but quickly became a star reporter. If there was a breaking story, she was on it.

When Ivan was meeting with his team, she was in a van speeding towards a gruesome murder case in Oakland.

A uniformed officer greeted the reporter and her cameraman, Dave Miller, as they jumped out of the White Ford van, satellite dish mounted on top. "Sorry Miss. Fisher, you can't go in there. He knew her name from watching TV.

"Why not?" she asked.

"Orders from the head detective, the crime scene is a mess. Trust me you don't want to see it anyway."

"See what," she asked.

"Well you see, the girl…oh tricky. I'm not allowed to tell you either."

"What can you tell me? I need something for 5 o'clock."

"Two dead, one male, one female, both white, in their residence. That's about it for now."

"Okay, thanks," Gwen told the officer.

A group of neighbors were standing in the street.

"Come on Dave, let's see what they know." She went over to interview the group of people standing around. As she did, Dave said "Rolling."

The news came on. Gwen heard in her ear, "You're the lead story."

She placed herself in front of the camera with the crime scene apartments behind her.

In her ear piece she heard the news intro. Co-Anchor Chuck Brimal said, "We have breaking news in

West Oakland near the MacArthur
Bart station. We go live to Gwen
Fisher. Gwen what can you tell us?"

Gwen looked directly into the
camera and put on her most serious
face. "Chuck, these apartments right
behind me have been the location of a
murder that can only be described as
something out of an Alfred Hitchcock
movie. I have been told that the
murder of the girl is so heinous; the
lead detective is not allowing anyone
to see the body. It is a double
homicide, a man and a woman.

This is my interview with neighbor, Dennis Pickford. Dave rolled the tape.

Gwen: Mr. Pickford, "What can you tell me about the couple?"

Dennis Pickford: "They were quiet and friendly. Never caused no trouble."

Gwen: "Any sign of dealing drugs?"

Dennis Pickford: "No, nothing like that. Tim had an East Coast accent, New York, I think."

Gwen: "Did you see anything unusual today?"

Dennis Pickford: "Just a lot of cops."

"Thanks Dennis, for some local insight.

Chuck, commuters should avoid the MacArthur exit from 580, the police action has it all bottled up. That's the story from here. This is Gwen Fisher in West Oakland, Chuck back to you."

***

When Ivan arrived home from his meeting, he turned on the TV news. He watched Gwen's report with rapt attention. Then he called Rebecca, Merle and Rich.

The four met at Rich's house in Los Gatos. Rowena, after introductions, ordered them a couple of pizzas, then went out shopping. Rich often had these emergency tech meetings about some thingamajig or widget.

They were in his basement man cave with all TV sports stuff in one area and a side room with a round meeting table. The basement was hardwired to keep out any listening devices. This was Rich's favorite room for research and development for his digital hardware company.

Rebecca started the meeting. "Now that you know the dream is real Ivan, how are you feeling?"

"Actually, relieved. This is all so intense, but at least I'm not going crazy."

Rebecca said, "Nobody thought you were going crazy."

"Really, come on, don't tell me that. Even I thought I might be going a bit bonkers."

Then all admitted they had their doubts about his vision dreams.

"But, Rich said, "Merle and I believed you enough to develop a couple of little presents."

"You're kidding?" said Ivan.

Merle said, "Of course, it's what we do."

Rich said, "I developed this especially with you in mind."

Ivan said, "Looks like an ordinary cane."

Rich went on, "That's what I wanted it to look like. But you see these buttons on the side, watch."

He pressed the first one. A blade came out the bottom. He pressed it again and the blade disappeared. "Cool huh- maybe you can use some of your high school fencing prowess."

"Thanks Rich, nice gift." Ivan said.

Merle said, "I have a new app on your chip. I think it will be very useful, Rich, turn out all the lights. Ivan, what do you see?"

"Amazing, it's like I have on night vision goggles."

Rich said, "This guy is dangerous. We just want you safe. Watch your back, Ivan."

That night Ivan had the dream that would move him into the shadows.

***

Gwen also had a dream. She was back in the age of Chivalry. A Knight rode up to her on a war horse. Both man and animal were dressed in black armor. The visor on the man's helmet was closed, covering his face.

He bowed his head and pushed his lance forward, tip just in front of her. She tied a white scarf to the lance. The Knight turned the horse, almost dancing. The whole scene came into her view. It was a tournament with hundreds of people sitting around a jousting arena. She could see the crowns on the king and queen.

Her knight, covered in black steel charged his foe, her scarf tied to his lance. She woke before the clash. That was an interesting dream, she thought as daylight peeked around her curtains. She looked at the book on the night stand she had been reading before sleep closed her eyes. *Ivanhoe* looked back at her.

Gwen's Eurasian look came from the union of her Japanese-American father, Joey, and Jewish-American mother, Linda Hathaway. Her mom had been a movie star and met her husband on the set of a World War II John Wayne movie. Joey played the enemy pilot who shot down the hero.

In the reality of World War II, Gwen's Japanese American grandparents spent the war as

prisoners in relocation camps. Gwen
and her brother grew up in Venice,
California, surfing the waves and
Gwen loved the LA lifestyle. But
when the San Francisco TV station
beckoned she settled in the East Bay
town of El Cerrito.

As she pulled herself out of bed
and into the shower, she thought
about her upcoming date with Ivan
with excited apprehension. She had a
wonderful crush on the former high
school teacher. She fondly remembered dancing with him. He was
a full foot taller than her. Her head

against his chest for the slow numbers felt divine. She had wanted to dance with him all night that night until his sudden collapse. She felt somehow bound to him.

Ivan arrived in a new ride, a Tesla all electric mount, environmentally correct, very cool looking, and expensive. He ambled over, sporting a cane, gave her a big hug and a kiss on the cheek. "Hi Gwen, you're looking lovely as usual."

She wanted to say, I just threw something on, but held her tongue. In truth she tried on three outfits before she settled on her blue short skirt, with a white shirt tucked into the leather shiny belt with a blue scarf matching the skirt. The two of them were dressed in complementary colors. He wore jeans, white shirt with a blue sports jacket.

"You're looking pretty good yourself. Do you need the cane or is that just you being dapper?"

"I'm glad you like it. I don't really need it but it helps me with my balance, you know, since the operation."

"And the new ride, very chic. Who are you?" She said with a laugh.

"Well I'm commuting now to Palo Alto. Got to stay green and I'm not on a teacher's salary anymore. Chez' Panisse okay for dinner?

"Sounds wonderful, you're not on a teacher's salary anymore?"

SmartWare pays better.

Ivan and Gwen talked and laughed through three courses of California-French, fresh delicious food. They conversed easily, like they had never been apart. Time flew.

Ivan looked at his watch. "It's 10:30 already. I was going to take you dancing."

"You'd better, you owe me a dance. It's not too late."

"Okay, I'm game. Let's find a club."

Just then her cell phone rang. She held up one finger. "Okay, I'm at Chez Panisse. Dave will be here in 10. Okay." She said into her phone.

"Ivan, I'm so sorry. That was work. I've got a breaking story. A woman has just been murdered in The

City just off Market Street. I'm afraid
duty calls."

"Oh no! Can I go with you?"

"No. sorry, you know, legal
insurance stuff. But you can follow."

As Gwen was waiting, Ivan
paid the bill and had the Valet get his
car. When the TV van scooped up
Miss Fisher, Ivan followed them
across the new span of the Bay
Bridge. The crime scene was already
marked with yellow tape.

Gwen talked to a police officer,
glanced into a mirror to apply lipstick
and powder any shiny spot that might

show up on camera and was ready to go. She heard Chuck on the earpiece say, "Now to Gwen Fisher in San Francisco." Dave pointed the camera. "Go," he shouted.

"Joan Walker, mother of two young children was assaulted by a homeless man, with a cardboard cutter. Unfortunately, she did not survive the attack. The perpetrator, Roger Meeker, is in police custody, That, Chuck is the sad story from just south of Market Street, downtown San Francisco."

Dave said, "Okay, you're clear."

Gwen spoke with Ivan. Neither wanted to go dancing.

"Should I take you home?"

"No, thank you, I still have some wrap up to get on tape."

They cheek kissed and said good night on what should have been a romantic evening.

Ivan drove home feeling overwrought and somehow guilty like he could have stopped the attack. It was all in his dream two nights ago.

Chapter 17   Best Man

Rich De Leone studied a twin of the chip that was in his buddy's head. He put it into a computer simulated brain, ran every test. It was working just as it should. It was designed to grab the faintest memories and act to restore the damaged neurons in the cerebrum. Just like each neuron's dendrite fires a chemical signal across the synapse to the next neuron's axon, the chip simulates the process, firing an electronic charge for each damaged cell. In the simulator it was working perfectly, just as it was in Ivan's brain. But he couldn't find any reasons for the dreams.

Einstein, in the theory of relativity said that time travels at a relative speed depending on different factors. Maybe his chip was picking up signals from the future? It almost made sense, he thought.

Rich and Ivan had been fast friends since their college days at

Berkeley. At 6 foot 8 inches, he
towered over Ivan, actually he
towered over almost everybody and
was wide as a diesel truck. On the
basketball court, he was the
unmovable object. He would plant
himself just outside the key by the
basket and Ivan, the unselfish point
guard would often feed him the ball
for his classic hook shot or follow to
the basket completing a give and go.
With two good outside shooters and a
decent center, the wins kept adding
up. The Cal Bears won two Pac 10
championships and made it all the

way to the Sweet 16 in their senior year. The two became inseparable on campus except in classes, with Ivan majoring in history and Rich engineering.

When Rich asked why a lifelong New Yorker would pick to go to college in California, Ivan shared the story of his uncle showing up at his high school with the young hooker. He figured California was far enough away to have that not happen again in his college years. Rich thought the story was hilarious and made sure all of Ivan's dates found out how his buddy lost his virginity.

Many years later, Rich asked Ivan to be his best man.

He said, "Of course. I suppose that means I organize your bachelor party."

"Yeah, and I've already decided what that should entail."

"Okay, lay it on me, as long as we don't get in trouble with the law or Rowena, especially Rowena."

"The big man laughed. Okay here's my idea, we go to Vegas and you invite your Uncle David. I've got to meet this guy, just to make sure you didn't invent him from your imagination."

"Dude, my imagination's not that good. But I haven't seen him in years. I have no idea what he's up to."

Rich replied, "Well then, let's find out."

Ivan said, "Okay, that's what you want, that's what you'll get. I guess Las Vegas is far enough away, neutral territory."

***

So, this is how Ivan found his Uncle David again and forgiveness. They hugged, talked, cried about the loss of a father and brother. Then the three men had a memorable time, but as Rowena would learn or not learn; *What happens in Vegas stays in Vegas.*

Chapter 18   Who Are You?

Rebecca listened as Ivan poured his heart out. He described the dream, then Gwen's report of the murder, twin images. "So do you think you could have stopped it?" She asked.

"Yes. Yes I do."

"How?"

"I know every detail."

"And why do you think it's your job?"

He looked at her and smiled.

"Why else would I have these dreams?"

"Why not call the police?"

"And tell them what?"

She had no answer.

"Next time I'll be there," he said.

"Let's hope there is no next time."

"Rebecca, we both know there will be."

"Ivan, just stay safe."

"Okay I will, just for you."

She looked at him with the dread of a mother watching her son going off to war.

***

The first time Ivan stepped out of the shadows and used his cane to save Kathy Linden, he wanted to be invisible, unseen. Ivan retreated feeling satisfied but disappointed. He had hoped staying in shadows, he would escape unnoticed. The secret was out, only his identity remained unknown. But for how long?

Channel 8 News ran the tease all day: Tune in tonight for the 6 o'clock news. See our own Gwen Fisher's interview with Kathy Lindon. Who is the Black Knight?

Gwen smelled a good story and like a bloodhound after an escaped prisoner she would follow her nose wherever it would lead. The fact that she was after a good guy bothered her a little but a good story was what TV news was all about. Unfortunately for her, Miss Lindon's interview turned out to be a bust. She had her back to her assailant and her rescuer.

She only saw him as he was walking away dressed entirely in black.

"Why did you call him the Black Knight?"

"When I asked him who he was he said he was the Black Knight," Miss Lindon said.

Then it was off to the county jail for Gwen, to find Kathy Lindon's alleged assailant, Michael Thompson and arrange an interview.

It turned out that he was no help in identifying the elusive Black Knight. She learned the prisoner never even saw the man in black, just felt the clubbing on the back of his neck and fell unconscious, until the police arrived. Apparently, Mr. Thompson liked being on camera. Without his attorney present he confessed to two other assaults.

Gwen turned the story around and made it about the confessions of Michael Thompson. Since she wasn't an agent of the government, it was determined a lawyer did not have to be present. His confessions and priors would put him away for life.

Ironically her failure to unveil the Black Knight would lead Miss Fisher to a different notoriety. She would win a prestigious BAMI award for this jailhouse interview.

Chapter 19   Date Night

Ivan and Gwen tried date three hoping for an uninterrupted evening of dancing. No nightmares had darkened Ivan's REM sleep cycle in days. He felt exhilarated. He parked the Tesla at the Oakland ferry for a romantic sunset ride to San Francisco.

Colors splashed across the Golden Gate like multiple rainbows set free to dive in the pacific. He gave and accepted the goodnight kiss they had missed on their Chez' Panisse night. It was worth the wait. Their bodies locked in anticipation of what might be.

"I see you are not using your cane anymore."

"Yeah, my balance is better."

In truth Merle and Rich came up with a better idea. A tai-chi sword that could telescope down and fit into his pocket.

They ate shish kebab, standing up at a Greek take out in the Ferry Building, sometimes kissing between bites. Uber took them to Polk Street and a dance club called, Hole in the Wall. The band, Bite Me, played John Mayer style rock 'n roll. Ivan and Gwen danced, danced and danced some more. Gay couples intermingled casually with the straights, a truly San Francisco experience.

Leading, he had her go under his arm, shimmy side to side, loop around his back, kick her heals to his sides, then the big finish, straddling him.

Out of breath, Gwen said, "You

know you dance way too well for a straight guy."

Ivan laughed. "That's what my only college dance class teacher told me."

It was Gwen's turn to laugh. "You took a college dance class?"

"Hey, can you blame me? I was the only straight guy in the class. I figured the odds were pretty good."

"Were they?"

"A gentleman never tells."

Gwen said smiling, "I knew there was something about you I liked." Then without the smile she looked into his eyes. "You are a gentleman."

"Thank you." Ivan said, meeting her eyes.

Taking her hand he suggested, "Let's take the cable car to the Fairmont and get a drink."

"Let's."

They threw on their jackets and went out into the cold foggy night air, her arm nestled in his, sharing body warmth. The California cable car line deposited the couple at the top of Nob Hill. The Fairmont loomed in front of them -- when he saw it.

His mouth dropped. Parked in front of the hotel was his Uncle David's restored 57 pink Caddy still sporting New York plates. Shocked and angered, Ivan led Gwen away. This can only mean *he* was here.-- Brian. Ivan did not want a reunion taking place with Gwen there.

"Ivan, weren't we going to the Fairmont?"

"I've got a better idea. We need a bay view. Let's go to that cute little bar next to the ferry building."

"Okay, I guess I'll go anywhere with you."

They both knew it. They were falling in love.

The goodnight kiss lingered. She was so temped to ask him up

No not tonight, she thought with regret.

Chapter 20   Target

Ivan fell back into dreamland that night. A Napa High tenth grade boy departed Target in late evening just after sunset in the Napa store's parking lot. Two young men, tattooed from head to legs, lurked in the twilight.

One's tat had 3 tears coming out of an eye, a sign that three of his comrades, or gangbangers, had been killed.

"Hey man we can get your dent out for 50 bucks." The shorter of the two said."

"No thanks, I don't have that much cash on me," said the kid.

"How much you got?" The two bangers moved to each side of their prey.

One took a suction cup appliance like a big toilet plunger and pulled out the dent. "There you go, man. I'll let you off for $20."

"I don't even have $20."

"Last chance before I fuck you up," The other one said brandishing a knife. "I don't care if I go to prison."

The boy reached in his pocket and brought up a $10 bill.

"Too little too late, motherfucker. That's for disrespecting me. Run!" He yelled.

The boy hadn't even felt the knife go into his side. His left hand moved to cover the hole. It was covered in red. "Help me!" he yelled, to an uncaring parking lot.

Finally the woman who parked next to the boy arrived and found him in a pool of blood. "Oh my God!" she exclaimed and called 911. Down on hand and knees, she tried pressure to stem the bleeding. Too little. Too late.

Two evenings later the Black Knight stepped out of the shadows, sword in his right hand. The felons walked up to the tenth grader. The boy looked like he could have been in one of Mr. Duncan's classes at Berkeley High.

The grin the taller gangster wore faded like the daylight, replaced by a face of surprise as the sky darkened. The sword reflected the last twilight. In silence the two tattooed villains departed, taking their evil elsewhere.

With shocked relief, the boy turned to say thanks, but the man dressed in black was already gone. The boy drove home, small dent still in his car. Mark Allen, the tenth grader, immediately facebooked and embellished his story about being saved by the Black Knight. The boy's story went viral.

Headline: San Francisco Chronicle

January 4, 2014

Who is the Black Knight?

Chapter 21   Tahoe Dreaming

As the Black Knight, Ivan had saved eight people in the first two months of the year. He shunned the notoriety, preferring to stay in the shadows, but a legend grew. Speculation propagated and rumors were cultivated like wine grapes in the Napa Valley.

He was everywhere but appeared nowhere on any camera. So did he really exist?

The dreams came at the average of one a week, giving him time to recover mentally before his next joust. He also had time for romance as he and Gwen continued to build on their relationship. President's day weekend plans for Gwen and Ivan included a trip up to the Truckee Inn to ski at Alpine Meadows and Squaw Valley. Putting chains on the Tesla did not strike Ivan as a great idea so he rented a four wheel drive Audi for the trip.

The weather turned unusually cold and a major storm set upon them despite the drought that had ruled California's climate the last few years.

They scooted Friday morning at the break of dawn to beat the weekend traffic up interstate 80. At Auburn the rain turned to big flakes of snow. By having the 4 wheel drive vehicle, they sailed past chain controls. Soon the white on white of snow falling on the granite shoulders of the Serra Nevada came into view. Four all season radial tires hugged the icy roadway as they climbed past forests of ponderosa pines, the highway switch backing up to Donner Pass.

As he drove up the mountain he so wanted to tell her his secret. About the mother who was carjacked and beaten to death by a young man while her baby slept in a car seat in back, soon abandoned by the roadside, only to be killed by a passing car. About the gay boy beaten to death in a high school bathroom. About the mother of three who was killed by a drunk driver. About the girl who was raped and left for dead.

He wanted to tell her how he had saved them all. Could he trust the reporter in her? Not yet, even when she speculated about the identity of the Black Knight. It was so hard to bite his tongue and not blurt it all out.

The town of Truckee is a throwback to the old west. The transcontinental railroad was built there in the 1860's and Amtrak and other trains still stop in a downtown that hasn't changed much since those pioneer days. The modern ski resorts are just fifteen minutes away.

They were both good skiers but this was the first time together. They decided to take on the lower slopes of Squaw Valley in the raging storm. He asked, "Have you ever skied KT 22?"

Her face lit up in a smile. "That's what I was thinking. It's a double diamond but a lower slope in the storm."

The chairlift was no fun. Snow attacked the couple while fifty mile an hour winds whipped. Masks hid their faces. Covered head to toe in the latest gear, the storm was bearable. As first turns in the virgin snow were made, they both screamed with delight, fresh powder! It was a wonderful day together laughing and playing like little kids.

Evening came, clouds hiding the moon and stars, the snow continued white fighting the black night's dominance. The spa at Squaw Valley provided much-needed massages and a soak in the outdoor hot tub.

"Does life get any better than this?" Gwen said, making a statement more than a question as snowflakes tumbled in a silent show. The River

Inn provided dinners fit for a king and queen. An appetizer of seared scallops and garlic was followed by steaks, garlic mashed potatoes and still crunchy grilled green beans. Fresh-baked bread delivered needed carbohydrates for the all-day skiers.

Back in Truckee the Audi tucked in behind the hotel, they went across the street to have a drink at the Bar of America as a band played country rock Willie Nelson style tunes.

Gwen had a look of please in her eyes.

"Okay," Ivan yielded, "one dance."

"Two," she insisted.

She just laughed as he put his arms around her.

Finally they were in their room, alone – together for the first time. Ivan's adrenaline flowed like that first run at the top of the mountain that morning. Gwen hid in the bathroom as she changed for bed and called out through the door, "I shopped for this just for you." She stepped out and sang, "Ta da."

She appeared in a black, sheer nighty with matching thigh high stockings. She took his breath away.

"My God, Gwen you are beautiful!"

Looking him up and down, she said, "Mr. Duncan, you're not so bad yourself, with your ripped abs and black silk boxers."

She closed the gap, was in his arms where he had wanted her to be for so long. They played, they danced, they made love.

Ivan slept and dreamed one of his dreams:

The woman's car broke down between Truckee and Tahoe city. A man in a blue pickup truck stopped. He turned his cell phone off at 10:22 PM and said to the girl with her thumb out, "Hop in." She jumped into the truck and said, "Thanks," her last word.

Behind a snow bank, he choked her until she stopped breathing and raped her still warm body.

Gwen woke him out his nightmare. "You made a funny noise like grunting. Are you okay? Having a bad dream?"

Ivan's heart was racing. It took him a few moments to figure out where he was. "Yes, bad dream." "You want to tell me about it?" "He took a deep breath, "morning – I'll tell you about it in the morning." He hugged her and held her close, safe.

At dawn with the curtains open, sunlight blasted into the room but the bed was still in shadows. They awoke, her arms hugging his back. He felt her coming to life. He didn't want to deal with the dream, he wanted her, needed her. Passion took control of

his body, seeing her, touching all of
her, smelling the lingering of her
perfume mixed with her mist, tasting,
languishing on the taste, hearing her
climactic screams, he moved into the
sunshine of her love, rhythmically, as
the bed came out of shadows and light
glistened off moist skin.

Laughing they fled into the
shower, soaping, playing, until there
was nothing left to clean. As they
dressed, Gwen asked, "Are you going
to tell me about the nightmare?"

He had been thinking, the assault would not take place until Sunday night. Gwen had to be back to work Monday morning. It seemed that fate was taking his secret from Gwen out of his hands.

"Gwen I have to tell you something important. Can I trust you?"

"Of course."

"Swear."

"You are kidding right."

"No this is too important and I know your reporter instincts."

"She was confused. I've been in your corner since you fell out of my arms last year."

"I know and I love you for it. Swear."

"Okay, if it's so important. I swear."

"Gwen, I am the person they call the Black Knight."

She laughed so hard she spit out her coffee. "Get out of town."

"I'm serious."

"No, how, why, no way." Tears started down her face as shock slapped her.

He told her the whole story, then asked for her help.

"If I just scare the rapist away, he'll still be out there ready for his next opportunity."

It only took her a second to say yes.

They went skiing.

***

The snow stopped, it was a black starless Sunday night when Ivan picked up the hitch-hiking girl. He asked, "Where are you going?" She couldn't be more than 16, Ivan thought, as he glanced at her.

She said, gum cracking, "Tahoe City, my car broke down, my name's Lucy." She half smiled at him.

"Lucy, do you like to go fast?

"In this car? Sure," she said as her smile grew.

"Buckle up."

He heard the click and the Audi exploded down the road. Ivan dropped her at the light and was back in the shadows in 16 minutes flat.

The blue pickup pulled in 10 minutes later. Gwen got in and pulled out a 38 special she had been packing in her purse since this whole serial killer episode began.

She said "Move a muscle and you lose your nose."

Ivan, appeared, not dressed as the Black Knight, and had the creep roll down the driver's side window. With a super smart phone in hand, that Rich gave him just days earlier, he took the driver's thumb print.

"John Carpenter, you have warrants out in California and

Nevada. I see the pick-up truck is stolen too. Nice." Ivan tied up the outlaw with knots he hadn't used since he was a boy scout and deposited him on the steps of the Tahoe City Sheriff's Office, a note taped to his chest. Just like that, Ivan and Gwen saved the girl and caught the killer.

After a kiss they drove home.

Chapter 22   Wizard

Ivan landed back at Merle's lab at UCSF. It was time for a physical and tune up. The two greeted each other with hugs. Rich would join them later to reprogram the chip.

Dr. Doggs started with his patient in the MRI machine. He studied output with great attention, like a college student studying for a tough exam.

Merlin "The Wizard" Doggs was one of the world's greatest brain surgeons. He had vast experience carving into heads with varied ailments. He was the go to guy for difficult cases and cutting edge progress.

Merle was among the first in the nation to experiment with Deep Brain Stimulation with Parkinson's patients.

Most people thought that his nickname came because of his expertise as a surgeon but it went back to his grade school days when he performed magic shows. People also, of course, would link him to the magician character in Camelot. His mother went into labor shortly after seeing the Broadway musical. His parents named the boy Merlin.

In middle school, bullies would try to make fun of his last name saying things like, "sit, you dog or roll over and bow wow." But after he would prank them with a magic trick, like a small explosion behind them with just a wave of his hand, they would respectfully call him *Wizard*. Not for long though, because he skipped eighth grade and went straight to high school.

His friends, then and now, called him Merle.

Seemingly lucky at life, Merle was not so lucky in love. He was married three times and had as many exes. "I love women a lot, maybe too much and too often. All three of my wives were good at keeping house, each kept one."

By twenty he had graduated from UC Davis and at age twenty-five he was a Board certified surgeon at UCSF. Presently at thirty he was dating a candidate to be wife number 4.

"Like medicine it's all about practice," he laughingly announced.

"How do you feel?" He asked Ivan.

"Good, real good."

"Well your tests look great."

Rich arrived. After ten minutes he said, "There is something different about you."

Ivan just smiled.

"Damn, Rich said, "You have tripped the night fantastic."

Ivan continuing his silence, smiled broader.

Rich said, "It's more than that, Damn, you're in love. I thought you were immune. Okay buddy, spill the beans."

"I've always been taught a gentleman never tells."

Rich let that go for about five second before the huge friend had Ivan in a head lock.

"Okay, you monster, if you let me go, I'll tell you about it. You guys are sworn to secrecy anyway."

Rich laughed and said, "I'll alert the Channel 8 News."

Ivan said, "You might have a problem with that."

"You SOB, it's Gwen." Rich said.

Words were not needed. Ivan just smiled at his two friends.

Merle said, "Good, she's seems like a great gal."

Ivan laughed, "To you, they all seem like great gals."

Then he told them about the weekend, leaving out the juicy parts.

He explained why Gwen now knew his secrets.

Rich said, "I know you're in love but do you trust her?"

"Yes, I do."

"Changing the subject, we have a new toy for you." Rich said. "It's a new type of sword. The handle has a "Star Trek" type phaser. Press right here on the handle and a laser beam silently blasts out rendering a foe unconscious. Point it at a car and it will kill the engine. Merle's magic and my software created it. Pretty cool isn't it?"

"I feel like James Bond with Q. Where is Miss. Moneypenny?"

Merle said giggling, "I think she's with Pussy Galore."

Rich teased his nerdy friend, "I think I know why you've had three wives."

***

Rebecca listened with a twinge of jealousy as Ivan poured his heart out about his growing love affair with Gwen. While self-assured and contented with her life, she wanted to share it with a partner. She wanted babies to love. Even living in San Francisco, where gay men might outnumber the straight, Rebecca had her share of dates and even lovers but finding *the one* proved elusive. She smiled and said, "Sounds like you and Gwen are lucky in love, I'm happy for you." She really was.

Chapter 23   Rowena Salsbury

During Ivan's summer vacations from teaching, Rich was the perfect travel buddy. They started with a Kerouac style road trip across the U.S. followed by Hawaii, Vietnam, and then Italy, where Rich De Leone was treated like royalty.

Four years before the aneurism, the two friends went to England to find Ivan's Father's English Literature legends and try to create a few new legends of their own along the way. Most people assumed Ivan's mom, being from Siberia, gave him the common Russian sounding name. His father actually named him Ivanhoe, which, of course, the modern American boy shortened.

Rich and Ivan toured England on their own with a preplanned itinerary. They started with Oxford where the late Professor Duncan completed his PHD.

The ghost of Louis Carol's Alice still seemed to haunt the

campus. Also a school favorite, were Sir Walter Scott's manuscripts, the author of Ivanhoe and the man responsible for the Robin Hood character.

From there they jumped to Sherwood Forest, then on to the Roman city of Bath. Next, to Stratford on Avon, William Shakespeare's home. A performance of Hamlet was mandatory. Finally, returning to London on the 4th of July, where England celebrates each year with the tennis tournament at Wimbledon.

The two tennis hackers cued up for tickets to get into the grounds for the outer matches. On line behind them were two of the prettiest women Ivan had ever seen. The one standing next to him was at least six feet tall, with a white short tennis skirt that showed off long powerful legs. Her sleeveless top revealed arms that would say on the court, don't mess with me. But it seemed her blue eyed smile could melt the hardest heart.

Ivan laughed when he asked, "Do you come here often?"

Her blond ponytail bounced as she turned toward him and said, "Come on Yank, I hope you can come up with a more clever pickup line than that."

Rich bailed him out, "Sorry his English doesn't translate that well on this side of the pond, he is from New York, not York."

She laughed at that and came back with, "What beanstalk did you climb down from?"

"Nice giant reference. I usually get, How's the weather up there?"

The ponytail bounced in front of Ivan to Rich and her hand touched his arm. "My name is Rowena and that's Catherine. You're not only tall, you're cute." Just a touch of blush came to her cheeks.

"Rich, I'm Rich." He blurted out, intimidated by the lovely woman apparently coming on to him.

"You are? Wow, tall, cute *and* rich. What else could a girl ask for?"

"No, I mean that's my name," Rich said, totally flustered.

"Rich, I'm messing with you." But she kept her hand on his arm like she was claiming a prize.

The line moved and the green grounds of Wimbledon opened for them, the last major natural lawn tournament in the world. Ivan said, "Look at that, grass, grass and more grass. It would be fun to play on that stuff."

Rowena said, "That could be arranged. What are you guys doing tomorrow?"

"It appears we will be playing lawn tennis with you two." Ivan said.

That is how Rich met his future wife.

The four of them had a fun day together on the hallowed grounds of Wimbledon. The highlight was watching Serena and Venus Williams win their doubles match.

The next day, Catherine and Rowena paired to easily defeat the two boys in their first match of English lawn tennis.

The girls were really good, almost professional players, while the guys just dabbled at the game. The women beat them royally.

Catherine, who had a boyfriend, was long gone after tennis.

Rowena became their unofficial London tour guide. Ivan watched his friend fall in love. But he never felt like the odd man out. Rowena had enough love for the two of them. By the time she came to visit in the States, Ivan felt like he had gained a sister.

Chapter 24   Coach

Gwen reported to work the Tuesday morning after the ski trip and was immediately sent out to another murder scene. A prostitute was skinned alive. Ivan watched her description on the television, with a look of disgust on his face. This homicide had Brian Gilbert's insidious signature all over it. Why didn't he see it in his dreams? He had been out of town and missed his opportunity to save the woman and take on his nemesis. He tried to weigh the girl saved in Tahoe to the woman dead in San Francisco. It did not compute.

He wanted Brian captured, to settle a personal score. Both Gwen and Ivan knew who perpetrated this wicked crime but the police found no evidence. Again this serial killer covered his tracks.

Comparing notes that night, they looked for a way to stop him.

"I think I have an idea." Ivan said, "I know this guy. He is New York thick and through, wouldn't leave Manhattan except to take the subway to the Bronx to watch the Yankees play. Brian would never leave New York unless he had to get out of town. Either he is worried about the cops or he pissed off the wrong guy and there is a hit out on him. Do you know a detective you can trust?"

"I think so, but my being a member of the press, my relationship with him slightly adversarial.

Jacob West, he's honest, smart and is on the homicide unit."

"Good, tomorrow I'll look up a couple of Uncle David's guys. You see if your detective will check with NYPD."

They made love, taking their time, bodies flowing like ocean waves dancing on the shore. Passion spent, Ivan curled next to Gwen, his front holding her back. A whisper reached her exposed left ear as if he was telling her a secret, "I love you." The secret would keep, she was already asleep.

That night a different story would play in his head. The former basketball coach watched as two of his boys, sophomores from his last year, now seniors, verbally and then physically assaulted a girl.

When Gwen looked at Ivan the next morning she could tell he was upset.

"You had another dream, didn't you?"

"Yes and it involves some former students." He filled in the blanks.

"What are you going to do?"

"What I always do, stop them, but I think the Black Knight can stay home this time," he said.

***

"Hey Jennifer, what's up? You want to party with us?" Michael Johnson asked, blocking the girl's path.

"No. I don't want to party, just want to go home." Jennifer Bishop said, fright creeping into her voice.

"What up Bitch? Think you too good for us?" Gary Summer moved behind the girl blocking retreat, his words slurring from alcohol.

"Please just let me past," Jennifer pleaded.

Gary reached out and pinched the girl's butt.

Ivan stepped out of the shadows. "Is this going to be the night that's going to ruin your lives, boys?"

"Coach, what you doing here?" Michael asked.

"I was just passing by. Lucky for you. You guys are probably too wasted to even remember this, but she and I will. So I repeat. Is this the night that's going to ruin your lives?"

Gary said, "Coach, we're not doing nothing. Just tryin' to have a good time."

"Gary don't you have a younger sister?" Ivan asked.

"So what."

"So what would you do to a guy who was doing this to your sister?"

"Yeah coach I'd fuck 'em up."

He looked like he suddenly realized what he was doing for the first time.

"If I were you I would apologize to Jennifer and hope she doesn't want to press charges for assault."

The smiles disappeared. Both Michael and Gary said, "Sorry Jennifer."

Ivan said, "Jennifer is there anyone you can call to come and get you?"

"Yeah, I can call my dad. Thanks Mr. Duncan."

"The boys and I will wait right over there by the corner. Are you okay?"

"Yeah I am now," she said, wiping a tear.

He turned back to the guys and walked them to the end of the block. He could keep an eye on the girl while he talked to the teammates.

"Do you two know how close you came to getting thrown off the team and maybe going to jail?"

"Why do you care? You left us and now word is, you drive a fancy new car," Michael said.

"You realize I left because I had brain surgery and almost died?"

"Yeah but you're okay now," Michael spit out.

"I see your point. You think I just left you for a better job." He had watched as Berkeley's varsity basketball team's record dropped each year since he left. Among other problems, the team showed a lack of discipline.

"Tell you what I'll do, Mr. Capriati's your coach now but if he will have me, I'll be his assistant for free."

"Wow, no shit? Oh sorry coach," Gary said.

Ivan said, "You know the rules when I coach. I'll bring your contracts with me when I come. No drinking and respectful behavior, you would be gone for this."

They were excited. Coach was coming back.

Chapter 25   Back to Berkeley

Sometimes dreams are just
dreams. Sometimes one's self-
conscious barks a warning like a good
watch dog or it can whisper so lightly
it is easy to ignore. Ivan's special
dreams were not normal. They were
technicolor productions even if events
took place at night. Blood ran red, car
colors beamed as if painted dayglow,
until now. Brian Gilbert started

haunting his sleep. He knew to be ready, his sword always with him. Ivan imagined him in the shadows, his shadows.

Ivan heard from Uncle David's former lieutenant who he had been friendly with back in NYC days. He told him Brian was in big trouble in New York from friends and foe.

"The guy just stepped on too many toes. But it's NY territorial, no one's goinna' follow him across the country. Good riddance to bad garbage. Know what I mean?"

Yeah I know, he's my problem now, he thought. Gwen informed Detective West about Brian. He promised to check him out.

Ivan went on with his life. He was welcomed back to the Berkeley High Basketball team as Joe Capriati's assistant. It didn't take Ivan long to identify the problem. Like many young teachers, Mr. Capriati wanted to be cool and have students and players like him. Ivan, Joe's former mentor, told the young coach, "You don't want to make friends with them. Sometimes they need a good kick in the ass. Get their attention and get their respect."

With Ivan running practices, Berkeley went on a winning streak. The boys remembered fundamentals and started moving the ball to get good shots. More importantly they tightened up the defense.

Also each player signed a behavior contract which Ivan modeled from his private school days. He reminded the players it was a privilege to play ball for Berkeley High. To be on the team, the boys were held to a higher standard. Their parents had to sign as well. Players knew Coach Duncan checked with teachers and had has spies watching, so if one or more screwed up, he somehow knew. That is what the player's believed. In reality, Ivan never had a student spy network. He knew students were like the mafia when it came to ratting each other out. Ivan just had a way of asking certain gossipy kids about the last weekend. An innocent question here and there gave him all the information he needed.

Chapter 26   Evil

Rebecca was having one of those days. First her car wouldn't start, so it was off to Muni where she had coffee spilled on her. A client missed an appointment without calling and her lunch date cancelled. So she was really looking forward to her 5:00pm appointment with Ivan.

At 4:40 Brian Gilbert walked into her office. He stood over her, evil grin on his face.

"Is there something I can do for you?" She asked.

"Yeah, you can spread those pretty legs and fuck me."

Rebecca picked up the phone to get building security. The line was dead. She could feel adrenaline pulse through her body, the fight or flight hormone. She thought about flight but the man blocked the door. Maybe I could get one good punch in and escape.

"That wasn't nice. I should introduce myself before I fuck you. Or should I skip all that and start carving?" He produced a large hunting knife, "Brian Gilbert at my ladies service."

She did her best to hide her fear. The psychopath had come for her. Then she remembered, Ivan was due here any moment. Delay she thought.

"Why do you kill people?" She asked leaning forward.

"You don't have to do that."

"Do what?" she asked

"The questions. You don't
need to shrink me. I hated my father
and loved my mother or was it the
other way around? Tell ya what, I'll
shrink you. What part of your body do
you like the most? My analysis is,
them lovely long locks. Yeah I cut
that off first. Then what next? Your
tits. They look like they would be
nice. Silly me, gotta cut the cloths off
first."

He took a step towards her and
threw out an insidious laugh.
Rebecca flinched and turned white.

"Scared? Don't worry. I'm not gonna start on you until after you watch me kill your friend Ivan."

Almost on cue Ivan walked in.

"There's our boy, Ivan Duncan. Long time no see. People might think you don't like me."

"I don't like you Brian. Anybody else you stabbed in the back besides my Uncle David?"

"Wow, you know about that. Good, I don't like you neither? But don't worry I didn't carve on your shrink yet, I'm going to kill you first."

Ivan unleashed his sword.

Brian said, "Oh look you got a bigger knife then me. Dumb shit, you never bring a knife to a gun fight."

Brian reached in his jacket pocket and pulled out a 45 semi-automatic complete with silencer.

"I'm gonna kill you slow, first your legs…"

Ivan pressed a button and Rebecca saw a blast of light from the phaser. Brian went down like a knight unhorsed in a joust.

Chapter 27   Winged Revenge

Detective West called Gwen out of courtesy to warn her,

"He will be out on bail soon."

"That is so wrong, the man is a psychopathic serial killer."

"Listen, Gwen you're preaching to the choir. I believe he is the guilty bastard but there is no forensic evidence and a first year lawyer gets Ivan's testimony thrown out as prejudicial. Rebecca was never assaulted. We charged the guy with malicious trespass. Freaking trespassing. Of course he makes bail."

"I just want time to get our people safe. Give me an hour."

"Sorry, not my call. Times up."

"Okay Jacob, thanks."

Gwen called Ivan, who called Rich, Rebecca and Merle. Only Rowena, who was down in Las Gatos unaccounted for, out of cell phone reach, was unprotected.

Unaware, she unplugged the phones to take a relaxing bath.

Ivan took off, driving the Tesla at full speed, leaving from practice in Berkeley, a full two hours away from her with Bay Area traffic.

Released in South San Francisco, Brian enjoyed the ride in Ivan's Uncle David's 57 Caddy, the one with fins. Maybe the most beautiful car ever made, he thought, knowing he had a one hour head start. Since going to jail, he had the six friends watched. Round two was going to be different.

Gilbert entered the last hill going to the De Leone house. As the Caddy started up the switchbacks, Ivan was still twenty-five minutes behind. Automatic gears downshifted as the big pink convertible climbed higher. The road reversed itself going up the steep grade.

Sun ducked under the fog exploding in a prism of color, dispersing sunset to the west. One Monarch butterfly moved the opposite direction of the Cadillac, then two, then fifty. Brian, wrapped in the armor of General Motors, strove forward on his quest. He became engulfed in the swarm of migration of thousands of Monarchs, colors devouring colors until the bugs smashing against the windshield were so thick, they blinded the lifelong city man trying desperately to see the road up the hill.

One of the butterflies landed on Brian's nose and opened its wings covering Brian's eyes. That insect had migrated thousands of miles just to be in this spot at this time. Unable to see, Brian still charged forward.

The street switched back and the car left the road, tires grabbing desperately for traction that was not there. Momentum shifted and the big automobile became dead weight. It fell the first two hundred feet without touching anything. Outer branches of a redwood tree reached out and slapped the car on its downward flight. Five hundred feet later, Caddy met concrete, mashing pink painted metal on the road.

Gas tanks and friction met in a Newtonian gravitational formula and exploded into fire. The fire consumed Brian Gilbert like the devil taking his due.

Chapter 28   It's Magic

Ivan saw smoke next to the road at the bottom of the hill leading up to Rich and Rowena's home. Firemen must have just arrived as they beat back the flames. Not allowed to pass, he got out of the car to look around. Almost at his feet was a tail light attached to a pink fin unique to the '57 Cadillac.

A single sycamore tree flamed into its crown, a tribute to the sacrifice of the butterflies.

The fire department did a great job keeping the fire from moving into the woods.

Ivan again tried to phone Rowena. After three rings she picked up.

"Where in the world have you been?"

"I was taking a bath and didn't want to be disturbed. Why?"

Ivan laughed and laughed, then reported the day's news to the surprised Mrs. De Leone.

***

That night the whole group assembled at the house in Los Gatos, celebrating with a sense of relief. Ivan proposed a toast to those killed by the madman, starting with a tribute to his Uncle David.

"To the man who paved my way through puberty and made me a legend with my schoolmates."

Alcohol flowed and grass was "mowed" as six good friends cried and laughed at the emotional roller coaster ride that entangled their lives for the last few weeks.

Ivan took a quiet moment with Gwen in the hot tub to say "I love you," with her fully awake this time.

She raised her glass filled with Champagne and said, "You'd better love me because, I'm stuck on you like super glue." Their eyes met laughing, until tears of joy flowed.

***

Ivan did not dream in technicolor that night. Instead he had a normal dream about Monarch butterflies. He wrote it down to ask Rebecca about it at their next session. Then went back to sleep.

He awoke to an altered world where Rebecca emerged from a guest room after sleeping with Merle.

No, he thought, this is just too good to ignore.

"So Rebecca, was last night magic?"

"Abra cadabra, Ivan, abra cadabra!" Rebecca declared, a satisfied smile planted on her face.

With a puff of smoke, Merlin, the Wizard, appeared smiling like the cat that ate the canary.

Chapter 29   A Hideous Plan

Ivan's life returned to normal, pre-chip normal. During the week, Ivan would live in Gwen's Berkeley apartment, allowing him good logistics to Coach. Weekends they would stay with Rich and Rowena when not off skiing. The special dreams did not come.

Merlin checked Ivan's head and Rich checked the computer chip and both reported everything was okay. Rich gave a hypothesis that the chip had gotten the kinks out and was now working the way it was designed, with no strange dreams. Without the distraction, Ivan and Gwen started hinting about a life together.

Merle and Rebecca continued to be an item. When Ivan asked her if she was now a candidate for wife number four?

She said, "Oh no, no, no, no, a leopard doesn't change its spots. Merle will always look for greener pastures on some other lawn. I'm not falling in love, just in it for the fun and the sex. You know he really is a magician."

Ivan said, "Careful, good sex like good drugs can be addicting."

And they laughed.

***

San Francisco Chronical Headline Whatever happened to the Black Knight? Remember when he was everywhere?

***

    Summer vacation found the six friends on a Greek Island. Upon returning, Ivan's first technicolor dream in months appeared. But it didn't make sense, looking more like a rough cut of a movie than a finished product. It started with an image of the Trade Towers going down.

    Out of the rubble, his father said, "Everything in your life's experience has led up to this. That is why I named you Ivanhoe; you are a hero. You can handle this with help from your friends."

Gwen, Rich, Rowena, Rebecca and Merle sang the Beatle's song, "You get by with a little help from your friends."

When Ivan woke up, he didn't wait for follow up. He called Merle first and explained his dream.

The Wizard, after laughing said, "I hoped you were done with those things. I guess not. It would appear fate has another game for us to play. Let's get the team together. We'll meet tonight after work."

Then, Ivan went to watch the Cal football team practice. Four of his former basketball players now played football for the Bears.

He looked over at the stadium and had a premonition that was visceral. Something from his dream would happen here. He started scouting like the soldier he once was, looking for weaknesses and strengths.

The group of friends met that evening knowing little. Rowena became secretary, taking notes. Ivan presented not just fact but premonition about the Cal stadium.

That gave them a place to start. They all agreed to do whatever was necessary to meet the still unknown crisis. They had Brian to thank for getting everyone's attention heightened.

***

A jet crashed into Memorial Stadium on the University of California's Berkeley Campus in Ivan's next special type of dream. He woke up stunned, "What in the hell was that?" He heard himself say out loud.

Ruminating, he figured the Berkeley stadium was an unlikely Al Qaeda target. Who had a motive? There's always Stanford, he thought with a chuckle.

Gwen with her reporter's instincts and experience came up with a possible answer. She started by googling Berkeley in the news. Next she eliminated most articles one by one, including Fox News ramblings about liberal Berkeley's evil ways.

The second day of research,
reviewing obscure stories, she found
something reported in The Seattle
Post-Intelligencer. A Christian
Fundamentalist preacher with a small
town cult following, railed against
San Francisco's "faggot" population.
He believed the devil's headquarters
was in Berkeley. The article
mentioned that the preacher, Lance
Moore, flew fighter jets in the USAF
until dishonorably discharged for
physically attacking a Black Muslim
Minister and a lesbian couple on the
same day, December 7[th,] 2012.

Gwen imported video of one of Moore's sermons. He was garbed in a hooded white robe almost looking like a member of that other mock Christian organization, the Ku Klux Klan. The small church was filled with about fifty loyal followers.

"My brothers and sisters, out there," he waved his arms out and back. "Out there is evil. Out there is Sodom and Gomorra. Out there is the Devil's workshop. Out there, is a place where men lie with men and women lie with women. Out there, sodomy prevails.

.

"All over our once great nation the snake crawls on its belly, ready to entice Adam and Eve to taste forbidden fruit. Out there, is San Francisco, where faggots march with pride, insulting good Christians like you and me.

"I tell you, they are infecting the nation, turning it into the Welfare States of America not the United States. Out there, they are turning us into the disunited states. Where is this disunion disseminated you may ask? Where does the Devil have his

headquarters to spew his dis-
information? Are you ready to hear
the word of God?"

"Yes." shout the people in the
church.

"I said, ARE YOU READY?"

"YES!"

"The devil speaks though the
pseudo-intellectual professors at the
University of California. Out there, at
the haven of demented thought,
Berkeley, California. Brothers and
sisters time grows short, we must
soon strike out at the Devil."

"Wow," said Ivan, "Sieg heil."

"Wow, indeed," said Gwen.

***

A third dream finally allowed Ivan to see the attack clearly. There were two parts to the incident.

A charter jet left Spokane just before sunset on December 6, 2014 with a total of sixty-two people on board, including Lance Moore, the pilot.

The Big Game, Cal vs Stanford, was televised that night, 65,000 in attendance. The jet lumbered out of the north and splashed down into the stadium, an exploding fire ball spreading faster than crowds could flee. Thousands died and thousands more casualties overwhelmed East Bay hospitals.

Moore's brother, Chandler, arriving earlier by bus, hid atop the bell tower on campus.

He launched the second part of the attack at eight o'clock in the morning, on Sunday December 7th. He used a sniper rifle to pick off people crossing below. With the mess at the stadium, police were glacially slow to respond.

Many more were added to the list of dead and wounded until a police helicopter could be sent with a tactical unit aboard to take out the sniper.

Chapter 30   Alternative Landing Sight

The *royal court* of three nobleman and three ladies met at Richard De Leone's castle like mansion in Los Gatos. They had to hatch a plan to stop Lance Moore and his younger brother.

Rich started, "Why not just call the police or FBI?"

Gwen said, "And tell them what? My boyfriend had a dream. How did that work with Brian Gilbert?"

Ivan asked, "Merlin, you're the magician, any ideas?"

"Yes, it'll be the biggest illusion anyone has ever seen and by far larger than anything I've tried before.

We need to create the illusion of another football stadium somewhere else and somehow steer Moore's plane to it."

Ivan asked, "Could you do that in two days?"

Merle responded, "I'm not sure if I could do this in two years but with a computer genius, we have a shot."

Rich asked, "What do you need me to do?"

"Two things. One, create a computer game board of the Cal football field and project it at a different spot. Two, make a phony GPS for the stadium and somehow sneak onto the plane and substitute it for the real one," Merle said.

"And do it all before the jet takes off." Gwen reminded them.

Rich smiled, "This is just the type of challenge my team loves. If we get it done, who delivers the GPS?"

"Sounds like a job for the Black Knight." Ivan volunteered.

"Except you're needed here to stop Chandler." Rowena said, "Let me do it."

Rich said, "No way. Too dangerous."

"What for a woman?" Rowena said. "Dammit honey, you men don't get to have all the fun."

Rich looked at Ivan for support. He shrugged his shoulders. "You know that woman's going to do what she's going to do. You know better than to try and stop her."

"What about me?" Rebecca asked.

"That's easy," Merle said, "You know any good magician needs a lovely assistant and this is the biggest trick I've ever tried. I'll need all the help I can get. I need you."

Rich and his team went to work. They had the advantage of not starting from scratch. Overhead views of the new home of the Cal Bears had been taken by the Goodyear Blimp and others. The crew loaded stills and moving pictures into the computer and broke them down to pixels. By the end of the day, three dimensional views were ready for Merlin to do his wizard magic.

Where to put the fake stadium became the next question. Wildcat Canyon was a unique site for Memorial Stadium.

Merle was counting on the probability that Lance Moore, feeling the way he did about the place, had never been there. So, where was an open space close to the University? There was a possibility but it was as different from Wildcat Canyon as one could imagine.

Just four blocks south of the campus, was People's Park. An open space that had been fought for by the hippies and students against the University of California administration; who wanted to pave it and turn it into a parking lot.

Many marches and tons of tear gas later, the park remained mostly as a crime infested homeless camp.

***

The day of the attack Merle released some five gallons of gasoline around the park and posted signs of a gas leak, to keep people away. Next, he and Rebecca placed light beaming projectors around the park.

"Well sweetheart, ready for some magic?" Rebecca turned two thumbs up. He flipped the switch.

People's Park at ground level lit up like a super complex Grateful Dead style light show but the view from the air gave the illusion of a game from Memorial Stadium, home of the Cal Bears.

***

Up in Spokane, Washington, Rowena pretended to walk confidently across the tarmac. She didn't feel confident, for all her bravado in the meeting. She was not some British spy and was a nervous wreck. Making sure she was alone, she jumped on the chartered jet and switched out the GPS, slipping the old one in her pocket. Turning to leave, she saw Lance Moore climb aboard.

"What are you doing here?" he asked.

"Me? I'm with the insurance company."

He looked at her skeptically.

"Okay, but sorry, it's too late to leave now. You will have to ride down with us."

Nice choice of words, great, I had to volunteer to be the brave one, now what do I do?

Church people boarded. Sixty-five people excited, laughing, like they were going for a day at the beach. It made her wonder why these people would blindly follow this guy. A woman about thirty-five years old sat down next to her. She smiled and said, "This is my first time going to California and my first time protesting anything ever."

Holy shit! They don't know.

The jet thrust down the runway picking up speed, effortlessly lifting into the air.

"Good morning fellow revolutionaries. This will be the beginning of our great rebellion. Tomorrow is December 7, the anniversary of Pearl Harbor. Let's go take back our country."

Rowena bee lined to the restroom, out came her cell and she had Rich on the phone in an instant, spilling the whole ugly story.

Rich thought for a moment, then said, "If he is determined to crash, we can't stop him. Even if you use the phasor I gave you, who could fly the jet? Take your belly chute and jump."

"Rich, you ever tried to jump from a jet going 500 miles per hour?"

"Un…no… oh," Rich stammered.

"I love you honey, but sometimes you're such a nerd. Never mind, I think it's time for me to play sexy stewardess. Bye," she said, with a determined look on her face.

Before leaving the restroom she checked her makeup, unbuttoned the two top buttons and walked into the cockpit and locked the door. She leaned in, touched his neck and using her sexiest English accented voice whispered in Lance's ear, "You know we have never been formally introduced."

Lance looked confused, then smiled, "No we haven't."

He reached up and put the plane on auto-pilot, then she blasted him with her phasor. Lance Moore was out cold falling from the captain's chair.

Rowena checked the flight pattern. They should be close to Portland. She called the tower.

"Mayday, Mayday, charter jet to Portland tower, come in please. non-pilot speaking."

"Portland tower to charter jet, I have your position. What is your present situation?"

"Suicidal pilot is out cold and I want to try and land this thing."

"Have you ever flown a plane before?"

"Small ones, not jets."

"Landings?"

"A few, my grandfather flew spitfires in WWII. He took me up often and he let me fly and land a few. My husband has a small jet and I've watched his pilot land a few times."

"Those were boats, this is a ship. I'll get the traffic out of your way. We have a trainer standing by, we have a glide path for you, just follow it. Okay I'm turning you over to Jack Paluas, good luck."

"Rowena, hi I'm Jack this is going to be a piece of cake. Really, no sweat. Ready to take control?"

"Let's get this party started Jack."

"All right I'm going to get you used to the yoke. Turn off the Auto-pilot."

"Done."

"You are now ready for some shallow dives and climbs."

"Jack, I'm ready. Let's land this puppy."

"Good keep that sense of confidence and good job moving up and down. Now turn the wheel and come to 320 on the compass. Very good. Do you see the glide path?"

"Yes, I see it Jack. I see it!"

"Great, follow it down. I'll tell you if you get off the line. Next throttle down slowly to 300 MPH. and lower the landing gear. A couple words of caution as we go on. Don't throttle down too fast or you'll stall, this is really important, when the wheels hit the ground stay off the brakes. It's a long runway. So let it roll and use the reverse thruster. Can you find it?

"Yes, I see it."

"Good, remember, NO brakes until I say brake. Now, down to 250 MPH."

"I hear you loud and clear oh captain, my captain."

Five minutes later Rowena bounced the plane hard but rolled it down the runway. She hit the reverse thruster and finally Jack yelled.

"Brake, easy does it."

The jet crawled to a stop as unneeded emergency equipment screamed to its side.

"Yes!" she shouted.

Only then, Rowena informed the passengers of the whole situation and why they were still alive. Then she called Rich and told him about the landing.

Chapter 31   Murphy's' Law

As the passengers deplaned and were ushered into a special wing of airport security, "Murphy's Law," took hold of Portland's Airport. The law states, "What can go wrong, will go wrong."

In their haste to get everyone off the plane, airport police neglected to secure the unconscious Lance Moore. The control tower went through a needed shift change. So when Lance Moore came too and asked for runway clearance, they gave it to him. He was flying on his way to Berkeley with no one the wiser, when twenty minutes later a lowly underpaid aircraft worker approached Rowena. She was being interviewed by Portland Police.

"Excuse me Miss but do you know where your plane went?" The man asked.

"You're kidding me right?" She said jumping to her feet.

"Well…er… no."

As she took out her cell phone, the police officer said, "Sorry but you can't use that now."

"Really, do you want 65,000 people to die because I can't use the freaking phone?"

The officer actually thought about it before he said, "Go ahead, I guess it's okay."

Rowena speed dialed Rich. When he answered she said, Michael is on his way, get ready.

"How is that possible?"

"I have no idea, but the guy is probably half way there."

"Wow we were just going to take it all down."

He put a hand to cover the phone, and yelled, Merle, Lance is on the loose with his plane and on his way, get ready. It's Abra Cadabra time!"

Merle switched on the power and People's Park again became a cascading light show that from above looked like an aerial view of Memorial Stadium.

Just ten minutes later jet engines roared above, far off course for Oakland or San Francisco

Airports. Rich looked up, to see the jet circle once and dive, plunging into the mostly empty space of a never built parking lot.

Safely behind a shield of steel, Rich dialed 911 as a giant fireball rose above Telegraph Avenue.

An old former hippy stoner said, "Far out man, best light show ever!"

Merle disappeared in the chaos that followed.

***

Ivan beat Chandler Moore up the bell tower and when he was confronted by the Black Knight's sword against his neck he simply surrendered, saying, "It was all my brother's idea. I really didn't want to kill nobody."

It was almost too easy.

Total casualties that day, 10 dead, 104 injured and 1 missing.

Total saved by actions of the Black Knight and friends 34,532 not killed, 24,602 not injured

That was the last time anyone saw the Black Knight.

Dreamland had almost ended.

Postscript

Ivan and Gwen planned a spring Tahoe wedding. Rich took a turn as best man. Instead of confronting Vegas' wildlife, the boys took an African wildlife safari. De Leone met the lion.

Gwen's bridal beauty shined through snow flurries. Ivan wore black tie.

Abra Cadabra, at the wedding, Merlin reappeared magically with wife number four, Sonya, a former

Russian ballerina, who had danced with the Bolshoi.

Ravishing Rebecca finally found love with Rachael, another psychologist she met at a Miami Conference. They adopted twin two year olds. Ira and Joan became the apple of both mother's eyes.

***

Just one month after an English country side honeymoon, Gwen was with child.

One last dream had illuminated Ivan's nights in England. After the dream, he used the phaser button to bury his special sword to the hilt, in a boulder made of quartz, like the silicon chip in his head. The sword sits imbedded, waiting un-pulled, in the rock at Salisbury Castle near Stonehenge.

It turned out that Rowena's family was related to the Royal family and had once upon a time lived in the castle. That gave Ivan access to the legendary Stone.

***

Ivan knew evil lived in the
hearts of men waiting in the shadows
in the black of night.

***

Ivanhoe and Guinevere would
dub their son Arthur.
A name fit for a knight
engaged in the cause of chivalry and
the nobility of a once and future king.

The Books of Nathaniel Robert Winters

Something for everyone:

Young adult:

Roger Raintree's 7th Grade Blues
A modern early teen adventure with relevant lessons to be learned in each chapter.

Young Adult and adults that have a love of dogs:

Finding Shelter from the Cold
Ice Age fictional story about wolves becoming dogs.

Its source was an ABC nature film using DNA evidence, will remind the reader of Jack London's:
Call of the Wild
Adult Novels:

The Adventures of the Omaha Kid- Romance, adventure, sports, triumph and tragedy

Penngrove Ponderosa- Story of Sonoma State students in the early 70's—sex, drugs with the shadow of Vietnam in the background

Sci-fi: Adult

Past the Future—Space ships, baby factories, Clones, Time machines just for starters.
Will Dave save the world?

Poetry and short stories:

The Poet I Didn't Know

Daydream Diversions

Memoir with fiction added

Rumors about my Father
Depression, Prohibition, Gangsters,
WWII

No Place for a Wallflower
Iola Hitt's WWII Story

The Legend of Heath Angelo
Story of Nature's Hero

Made in the USA
Middletown, DE
25 June 2022